ASTERIX AND THE CAULDRON

TEXT BY GOSCINNY

DRAWINGS BY UDERZO

TRANSLATED BY ANTHEA BELL AND DEREK HOCKRIDGE

*Hodder
Children's
Books*

a division of Hodder Headline plc

Asterix and the Cauldron

Copyright © Dargaud Editeur 1969, Goscinny-Uderzo
English language text copyright © Hodder and Stoughton Ltd 1976

First published in Great Britain 1976 (cased) by Hodder Dargaud Ltd
This edition first published 1981 by Knight Books, Hodder Dargaud

ISBN 0 340 26468 3

20 19 18 17 16 15 14 13 12 11

Published by Hodder Dargaud Ltd,
338 Euston Road, London, NW1 3BH

Printed in Belgium by Proost International Book Production

The year is 50 BC. Gaul is entirely occupied by the Romans.
Well, not entirely… One small village of indomitable Gauls still
holds out against the invaders. And life is not easy for the
Roman legionaries who garrison the fortified camps of
Totorum, Aquarium, Laudanum and Compendium…

a few of the Gauls

Asterix, the hero of these adventures. A shrewd, cunning little warrior; all perilous missions are immediately entrusted to him. Asterix gets his superhuman strength from the magic potion brewed by the druid Getafix...

Obelix, Asterix's inseparable friend. A menhir delivery-man by trade; addicted to wild boar. Obelix is always ready to drop everything and go off on a new adventure with Asterix — so long as there's wild boar to eat, and plenty of fighting.

Getafix, the venerable village druid. Gathers mistletoe and brews magic potions. His speciality is the potion which gives the drinker superhuman strength. But Getafix also has other recipes up his sleeve...

Cacofonix, the bard. Opinion is divided as to his musical gifts. Cacofonix thinks he's a genius. Everyone else thinks he's unspeakable. But so long as he doesn't speak, let alone sing, everybody likes him...

Finally, Vitalstatistix, the chief of the tribe. Majestic, brave and hot-tempered, the old warrior is respected by his men and feared by his enemies. Vitalstatistix himself has only one fear; he is afraid the sky may fall on his head tomorrow. But as he always says, 'Tomorrow never comes.'

THE SPRINGTIME CALM OF THE LITTLE VILLAGE WE KNOW SO WELL IS INTERRUPTED BY THE ANNOUNCEMENT OF AN OFFICIAL VISIT....

IF YOU THINK I'D TAKE A PART IN ANY GLEE WITH YOU, FULLIAUTOMATIX....

ANY MORE SINGING AND YOU GET TAKEN APART! WITH GLEE!

CHIEF WHOSEMORALSARELASTIX AND HIS MEN ARE ON THEIR WAY!

STRAIGHT AWAY A COUNCIL MEETING IS CALLED.

WHO IS THIS CHIEF WHOSEMORALSARELASTIX?

HE'S THE CHIEF OF A VILLAGE ON THE CLIFF TOPS. I DON'T LIKE HIM MUCH; HE'S TIGHT-FISTED AND HE'LL DO ANY SORT OF DEAL WITH THE ROMANS FOR MONEY....

HOWEVER, HE IS A GAULISH CHIEF! WHEN ONE GAULISH CHIEF MEETS ANOTHER GAULISH CHIEF, PROTOCOL MUST BE OBSERVED! LET PREPARATIONS BE MADE TO WELCOME HIM!

SOON AFTERWARDS...

NOW THEN, BOYS! DECORUM, DIGNITY, NOBILITY!

HERE HE COMES, CHIEF!

WOTCHER, MATE! BIT WARM, EH? HOW ABOUT A JAR?

?!?!

5

HAVE YOU COME ALL BY YOURSELF LIKE THAT?

OH, NO! HERE'S MY RETINUE.

?

WHAT THE... IT'S A CAULDRON!

YES, THAT'S WHY I HAD TO WALK. THERE'S NOT MUCH ROOM ON THESE SHIELDS.

YOU MEAN YOU GAVE UP YOUR SHIELD TO THIS CAULDRON? WHAT'S SO SPECIAL ABOUT IT?

IT'S FULL OF SESTERTII, BY TOUTATIS! COME OVER HERE... I'VE GOT SOMETHING TO TELL YOU.

2A

JULIUS CAESAR IS IN GRAVE FINANCIAL DIFFICULTIES. HE'S USED THE TAXES WHICH WERE GOING TO PAY HIS GARRISONS HERE IN GAUL TO EQUIP HIS ARMIES FOR NEW CAMPAIGNS...

I HEARD THAT CAESAR WAS ABOUT TO LEVY NEW TAXES, SO I PUT ALL MY PEOPLE'S SAVINGS IN THIS CAULDRON, AND I'VE BROUGHT IT TO YOU FOR SAFE KEEPING... I BELIEVE YOU DON'T PAY ANY TAXES?...

WELL, A TAX COLLECTOR DID SHOW UP ONE DAY... WE HAVEN'T PAID ANY TAXES SINCE!

DEAR ME!... I'LL NEVER FORGET HOW WE SHOWED HIM UP!

WHAT FUN WE HAD! REMEMBER WHEN...?

OH, DO STOP! HOHOHO!

YOU MEAN HE NEVER RETURNED?

THAT'S RIGHT. NO RETURN, NO TAX RETURN, NO TAXES!

2B

WHEN I KNEW WHAT THE ROMANS INTENDED TO DO I DIDN'T HESITATE! I GRABBED THE FIRST AVAILABLE CONTAINER, THREW OUT THE ONION SOUP SIMMERING INSIDE IT, AND FILLED IT WITH ALL MY SESTERTII!

AND I HAVE BROUGHT IT TO YOU FOR SAFE KEEPING! THE ROMANS WILL NEVER DARE TO LOOK FOR IT HERE!

BUT COULDN'T YOU HAVE HIDDEN THE MONEY... BURIED IT?

NO. THE ROMANS ARE ALWAYS EXCAVATING... THERE ARE SO MANY BURIED TAXES ABOUT THEY'LL PROBABLY BE GETTING DUG UP FOR CENTURIES TO COME!

IT'S A GOOD IDEA TO PREVENT THE ROMANS GETTING THEIR HANDS ON THIS MONEY...

IT IS, ISN'T IT?

..BUT I THOUGHT YOU WERE IN THEIR GOOD TABLETS... ESPECIALLY AS THE ROMANS LIKE PEOPLE WHO PAY THEIR TAXES REGULARLY.

WHAT?

YOU'VE NO RIGHT TO DOUBT MY PATRIOTISM! I MAY DO BUSINESS WITH THE ROMANS...

... BUT I ALWAYS MAKE THEM PAY TWICE THE PRICE I'D HAVE CHARGED MY GAULISH CUSTOMERS!

THAT'S GOOD!

VERY GOOD!

AND DO YOU DO MUCH BUSINESS WITH GAULS?

NO... THE ROMANS BUY EVERYTHING I'VE GOT TO SELL!

VERY WELL, WE'LL LOOK AFTER YOUR CAULDRON UNTIL THE TAX COLLECTOR HAS BEEN.

I WILL PUT IT IN THE HANDS OF MY MOST TRUSTWORTHY WARRIOR: *ASTERIX!*

I'M GOING TO PUT THE CAULDRON IN MY HUT.

HOW SILLY! FANCY THROWING OUT GOOD ONION SOUP TO MAKE ROOM FOR SESTERTII!

BUT OBELIX, WITH SESTERTII YOU CAN BUY ONION SOUP!

THAT'S THE POINT! WHY THROW OUT THE ONION SOUP WHEN IT WAS IN THE CAULDRON ALREADY?

I WILL STAND GUARD ALL NIGHT.

ER... THERE'S GOING TO BE A BANQUET FOR CHIEF WHOSEMORALSARELASTIX. I DON'T LIKE TO DEPRIVE DOGMATIX OF...

OFF YOU GO, OBELIX, OLD CHAP!

I'LL BRING YOU SOMETHING TO EAT!

WOOF! WOOF!

SOON AFTERWARDS...

YUM! SCRUNCH! GLOUP!

BY TOUTATIS! YOU EAT WELL!

EAT?... GLOUP!... EAT? I'D FORGOTTEN ALL ABOUT ASTERIX! I MUST TAKE HIM SOMETHING TO EAT!

YOU JUST SIT STILL! I'LL SEE TO IT! I'VE GOT A BIT OF INFORMATION TO GIVE HIM.

YOU'RE WELCOME... SCRUNCH!... I HATE BREAKING OFF BETWEEN TWO... YUM!... BOARS!

9

WE HAVE A DEBT OF HONOUR TO PAY, ASTERIX. CHIEF WHOSEMORALSARELASTIX ENTRUSTED A CAULDRON AND HIS SESTERTII TO US!...

GIVE HIM BACK HIS CAULDRON! THAT WILL PAY OFF HALF THE DEBT, AND...

SILENCE, OR I'LL HAVE THE VILLAGE CLEARED!!!

BANG! BANG! BANG!

IT WAS UP TO YOU TO LOOK AFTER THE CAULDRON, AND YOU FAILED IN YOUR DUTY. YOU HAVE BROUGHT DISHONOUR ON OUR VILLAGE. YOU KNOW HOW STRICT OUR LAWS ARE...

SAD AS IT IS FOR US TO TAKE THIS STEP, YOU ARE BANISHED FROM THE VILLAGE. YOU MAY RETURN ONLY IF YOU MAKE UP FOR WHAT YOU HAVE DONE.

I SHALL RETURN WITH THE CAULDRON FULL OF SESTERTII, OR I SHALL NOT RETURN AT ALL!

WELL SPOKEN, BY TOUTATIS! COME BACK WITH YOUR CAULDRON OR IN YOUR CAULDRON!

YOU KNOW THE MAGIC POWERS OF THIS POTION. IT WILL GIVE YOU INVINCIBLE STRENGTH! NOW GO, MY BOY, AND USE IT WISELY!

THANKS, O DRUID!

PARP

ASTERIX IS LEAVING! WHERE'S HE GOING?!!

LET HIM BE, OBELIX. HE IS BANISHED, BUT PERHAPS HE WILL COME BACK SOME DAY.

ARE YOU ALL OFF YOUR HEADS? LETTING ASTERIX GO OFF LIKE THAT, ALL ALONE? HOW DO YOU EXPECT HIM TO GET BY IF DOGMATIX AND I AREN'T THERE TO ADVISE HIM?

TAP! TAP! TAP!

MEANWHILE, NEARBY...

PALACE OF THE GLADIATORS

WHO'S FIRST?

LUCKY BLIGHTER! HE'S SURE TO GET THE PRIZE!

NEXT!

PAFF!

AND NEXT COMES THE NEXT...

CHLAC!

AND THE NEXT!

... AND RUNNING PRACTICALLY NECK AND NECK, THE NEXT...

AND THE NEXT!

AND THE NEXT!

AND THE NEXT!

TCHON TCHOC! PAF!

... UNTIL AT LAST...

RIGHT, I THINK THAT'S THE LOT. NOW YOU CAN PAY ME.

TCHAC!

WHAT DO YOU MEAN, PAY YOU? YOUR FAT FRIEND DID IN ALL MY GLADIATORS, YOU'VE DONE IN MY ENTIRE AUDIENCE, YOU'VE GONE AND RUINED ME AND YOU WANT TO GET PAID AS WELL?

TAP! TAP! TAP! TAP!

YOU JUST GIVE ME BACK MY MAGNIFICENT WORKS OF ART!

WHAT FAT FRIEND?

O, GIVE HIM HIS STATUETTES, OBELIX.

23

THIS IS OUR THEATRE. LET ME INTRODUCE MYSELF; MY NAME IS LAURENSOLIVIUS.

MY AIM IS TO TRANSFORM THE MODERN DRAMA! WE HAVE A MESSAGE! A MISSION! WE MUST SHOCK OUR AUDIENCES! JERK THEM OUT OF THEIR LETHARGY! IT MUST ALL BE NATURAL AND SPONTANEOUS!

NOW, LET'S GET ON WITH THE REHEARSAL! TAKE UP YOUR POSITIONS!

?!?

25A

ORGIES! ORGIES! WE WANT ORGIES!

HOLD ON A MOMENT! WHERE'S OUR DISGUSTED AUDIENCE? WHERE'S ALECGUINUS GOT TO...? YOU'RE LATE, DUCKY.

JUST COMING!

RIGHT. START AGAIN.

ORGIES! WE WANT...

YOU FORGOT ONE "ORGIES," DUCKY!

SORRY! ORGIES! ORGIES! WE WANT ORGIES!

STOP! THIS IS DISGRACEFUL! THEY'RE MAKING FUN OF US!

VERY GOOD, ALECGUINUS, VERY GOOD... IT MIGHT BE AN IDEA IF YOU THREW THINGS AT HIM...

NO, IT MIGHT NOT! THAT WOULD LOOK VULGAR!

25B

ALL RIGHT. NOW, YOU TWO WAIT UPSTAGE, KEEPING QUITE STILL....

...AND THEN I SHALL POINT AT YOU - YES, YOU, FATSO!...

HIS NAME IS OBELIX.

WHOSE NAME IS OBELIX?

...AND WHEN I GIVE THE SIGN, YOU COME UP TO THE FRONT OF THE STAGE, DOING A LITTLE DANCE, AND SAY SOMETHING: ANYTHING!

ANYTHING?

YES. THAT WILL BE THE END OF THE PLAY - A SPONTANEOUS CRY FROM THE HEART! JUST SAY WHATEVER COMES INTO YOUR HEAD!

BUT SOMETIMES NOTHING COMES INTO IT!

RIGHT! SEE YOU ALL THIS EVENING! WE MUST MAKE OUR MARK! WE HAVE TO GIVE THE PUBLIC WHAT IT WANTS: A MESSAGE!

BUT WHAT AM I GOING TO SAY? WHATEVER AM I GOING TO SAY!

OH, WHAT DOES IT MATTER? OUR CAULDRON IS THE IMPORTANT THING.

SO HOW ABOUT THE MESSAGE? DON'T YOU CARE ABOUT THE MESSAGE?

AND THAT EVENING, THE THEATRE FILLS UP WITH THE USUAL SCINTILLATING FIRST-NIGHT AUDIENCE! THE ROMAN PREFECT, THE OFFICERS OF THE GARRISON, ALL THE LOCAL BIGWIGS, IN FACT, EVERYONE WHO IS ANYONE IN CONDATUM.

I THINK THIS SHOULD BE ENTERTAINING, O PREFECT!

I HEAR THEY'RE QUITE DISGUSTING!

UNSPEAKABLE! I HAD A LOT OF TROUBLE GETTING SEATS!

THE SHOW STARTS...!

DING! DONG!

WHAT AN UGLY LOT YOU ARE! WE MAY BE UGLY TOO, BUT YOU'RE WORSE!

YAAAH!

IT'S SO DREADFULLY AUTHENTIC....!

ORGIES! ORGIES! WE WANT ORGIES!

STOP! STOP! THIS IS DISGRACEFUL! THEY'RE MAKING FUN OF US!

HE'S RIGHT!

NO, HE ISN'T!

THROW HIM OUT!

MUSEUM PIECES!

ROMAN RELICS!

THAT'S YOUR CUE! GO ON! GO ON, THEN!

I.... I'LL NEVER MAKE IT!

THINK OF THE CAULDRON!

NEXT DAY, STILL AT CONDATUM, AND...

STILL NOT A SESTERTIUS!

WE COULD SELL THE CAULDRON?

HOW WOULD THAT HELP FILL IT?

I SHALL NEVER, NEVER BE ABLE TO GO HOME TO OUR VILLAGE AGAIN!

THERE, THERE, ASTERIX! I'M SURE TOUTATIS WILL HELP US!

?!?

DONG! DING! TING!

I HATE TO SEE PEOPLE LOOKING SAD WHEN I'M SO HAPPY! I'VE JUST WON A PACKET!

DING! DING! DING!

DING! DING!

?!?!

HEY! WON IT? WON IT HOW?

AT THE RACES, MATE! AT THE RACES!

I ONLY HAD A FEW SESTERTII, I PUT THEM ON A CHARIOT, AND I WON!

WHERE EXACTLY ARE THE RACES?

IN THE HIPPODROME. FOLLOW ME; I'M GOING BACK TO MAKE ANOTHER PILE.

THERE, ASTERIX, WHAT DID I SAY?

THAT'S THE HIPPODROME. WELL, GOODBYE AND GOOD LUCK.

YOU KNOW, WHEN WE DO HAVE A BIT OF CASH FOR ONCE, I HATE TO RISK IT!

BUT THERE'S NO RISK! WE PLACE OUR BET AND WE FILL THE CAULDRON! THAT'S WHAT HE SAID.

ANY IDEA JUST HOW WE PLACE A BET, OBELIX?

MAYBE I COULD HELP YOU, FRIENDS!

LET ME INTRODUCE MYSELF: CONFIDENSTRA, I'M AN EXPERT. I CAN GIVE YOU SOME TIPS

YOU THINK WE COULD FILL OUR CAULDRON WITH YOUR TIPS?

SURE! IT'S LIKE THIS: THE RACES ARE FOR CHARIOTS CALLED QUADRIGAE, EACH DRAWN BY FOUR HORSES. YOU CAN BACK THEM EACH WAY...

... THAT IS, FOR A PLACE IN THE FIRST THREE, AT REDUCING ODDS, WHICH COMES TO TWELVE HORSES IN ALL...

?

BUT YOUR BEST BET IS TO BACK THE WINNER AT FULL ODDS: THE COLOURS ARE BLUE, WHITE, RED AND GREEN...HERE COME CLOSER...

?

PUT YOUR MONEY ON THE BLUES FOR THE NEXT RACE! I KNOW A COUSIN BY MARRIAGE OF THE AURIGA *. HE JUST CAN'T LOSE!

* CHARIOTEER

30ª

GIVE ME YOUR MONEY, AND I'LL PLACE YOUR BET... ALL I ASK IS HALF YOUR WINNINGS.

YOU'RE SURE HE CAN'T LOSE?

IT'S IMPOSSIBLE.... NOW, YOU GO INTO THE HIPPODROME WE'LL MEET AT THE EXIT.

30ᵇ

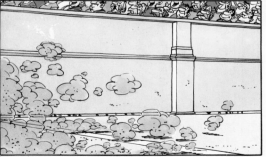

35

HARD LUCK, FRIENDS! BUT MY BROTHER-IN-LAW HAPPENS TO KNOW THE NEPHEW OF THE AURIGA OF THE GREEN CHARIOT IN THE NEXT RACE, AND HE...

WE HAVEN'T GOT ANY MORE MONEY! AND YOU TOLD ME IT WAS IMPOSSIBLE FOR THE BLUE CHARIOT TO LOSE!

IMPOSSIBLE IS NOT A GAULISH WORD, MY FRIENDS!

SIGH SIGH SIGH

SIGH

COME ON, OBELIX. I'VE STILL GOT A FEW BRONZE COINS LEFT. LET'S HAVE A BITE TO EAT.

SOON AFTERWARDS...

I RECOMMEND THE BOAR; IT'S VERY GOOD VALUE JUST NOW. PRICES HAVE FALLEN; BOAR ARE BEING SOLD FIFTEEN TO THE DOZEN AT THE MOMENT.

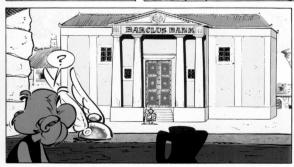
BARCLUS BANK

WHAT'S THAT? A TEMPLE?

NEAR ENOUGH. IT'S A ROMAN BANK. WHERE THEY KEEP THEIR GOLD.

HEY! YOU THERE!

ME?

YES, YOU! YOU LOOK TO ME LIKE SOMEONE WHO'S THINKING OF ROBBING A BANK, BUT YOU HAVEN'T GOT A HOPE!

THE BANK IS CONSTANTLY GUARDED. THE GUARD CHANGES AT NOON, AT SIX IN THE EVENING AND AT MIDNIGHT, AND THERE ARE MEN INSIDE ALL NIGHT...

THE GOLD IS KEPT IN A CELLAR WITH A HEAVY IRON DOOR WHICH HAS A SECRET CATCH HIDDEN IN THE ORNAMENTAL MOULDING...

TAP! TAP! TAP!

...SO DON'T GO GETTING ANY IDEAS!

SOON AFTERWARDS...

I DIDN'T LEARN ANYTHING. HE SAW THROUGH ME BEFORE I COULD GET ANY IDEAS.

NEVER MIND. WE CAN WATCH THE SENTRIES COMING AND GOING FROM THIS WINDOW.

WE SHALL HAVE TO TAKE TURNS KEEPING WATCH... WRITE EVERYTHING DOWN, INCLUDING THE TIMES...

AND FOR TWO DAYS AND TWO NIGHTS...

... OUR FRIENDS TAKE TURNS.

THERE WE ARE, OBELIX! I'VE WORKED OUT THE TIMES THEY CHANGE GUARD!

I NOTICE THAT ABOUT ELEVEN IN THE MORNING THE SENTRY LEAVES HIS POST TO HAVE A DRINK OF WATER AT THE FOUNTAIN...

ZZ. ZZZ

HAT'S OUR OMENT O ACT.

YAAAAWN!

LOOK, I'VE DRAWN UP A PLAN.

SCRATCH! SCRATCH!

SCRATCH SCRATCH!

BANK

ME

DOGMATIX

ROUTE TAKEN BY OBELIX

INN

35·A

DOGMATIX WILL KEEP WATCH ND WARN US IF THE SENTRY COMES CK SOONER THAN EXPECTED...YOU REAK DOWN THE DOOR...

I'M HIDING BEHIND THE THIRD COLUMN. I LEAP IN...

WE SHALL HAVE FIVE MINUTES TO CARRY OUT THE OPERATION BEFORE THE SENTRY GETS BACK. DURING THIS TIME, WE HAVE TO QUESTION THE STAFF AND FIND THE GOLD... GET IT?

NO.

RIGHT. NEVER MIND. WE PLOUGH INTO THEM, WE PICK UP THE CASH, AND WE BEAT IT.

I GET THAT!

TOIIIING!

GLUG! GLUG! GLUG! GLUG!

35·B

THIS DOOR WILL NEVER STAND UP TO THE MAGIC POTION!!!

BANG!

OH!

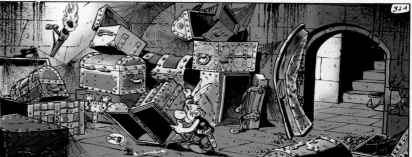

32 A

EY, WHAT ARE YOU DOING HERE? YOU WANT TO DEPOSIT MONEY, YOU HAVE TO DO IT AT THE COUNTER UPSTAIRS.

I DIDN'T COME TO DEPOSIT MONEY, I CAME TO TAKE SOME.

BANG!

OH, I THOUGHT IT WAS A BIT STRANGE!

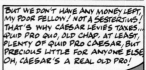

BUT WE DON'T HAVE ANY MONEY LEFT, MY POOR FELLOW! NOT A SESTERTIUS! THAT'S WHY CAESAR LEVIES TAXES.... QUID PRO QUO, OLD CHAP. AT LEAST, PLENTY OF QUID PRO CAESAR, BUT PRECIOUS LITTLE FOR ANYONE ELSE. OH, CAESAR'S A REAL OLD PRO!

COME ALONG, BELIX!

AND STOP THAT WHISTLING!

O.K.

32 B

IT DIDN'T COME OFF, THEN?

NO.

THE CAULDRON IS STILL EMPTY, AND I DON'T THINK WE'RE EVER GOING TO FILL IT...

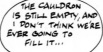

I SHALL TAKE THE EMPTY CAULDRON BACK TO CHIEF WHOSEMORALSARELASTIX AND EXPLAIN THAT I ALONE AM TO BLAME... THAT WAY, THE HONOUR OF THE VILLAGE WILL BE SAVED.

AND AFTERWARDS, WELL, I SHALL JUST GO AWAY FOR ALWAYS...

SNIFF! AND I SHALL ALWAYS GO AWAY FOR ALWAYS WITH YOU!

BOOHOOHOO! BOOHOO! HOOOOWWW!

SOON AFTERWARDS...

IT'S A GOOD IDEA TO TAKE THEM BACK THE CAULDRON. AT LEAST THEY'LL STILL BE ABLE TO MAKE ONION SOUP.

I'M SURE THAT WILL BE A GREAT COMFORT!

CONDATUM

AND AFTER A FEW DAYS' JOURNEY...

WE'RE GETTING CLOSE TO CHIEF WHOSEMORALSARELASTIX'S VILLAGE. IT'S ON THE CLIFF-TOP BEYOND THIS WOOD.

MAKE WAY! MAKE WAY THERE FOR THE TAX COLLECTOR, JULIUS CAESAR'S SPECIAL EMISSARY!

THIS IS OUR LAST CHANCE TO FILL THE CAULDRON!

GLUG! GLUG! GLUG! GLUG!

COME ON!

TRALALALA!

46